PRESENTED TO

_____

FROM

_____

Text copyright ©2004 by Melody Carlson

Illustrations by Susan Reagan

Cover and interior design: UDG | DesignWorks

Published in 2004 by Broadman & Holman Publishers,

Nashville, Tennessee

DEWEY: CE
SUBHD: AUTUMN \ THANKSGIVING DAY

ISBN 0-8054-2684-1

1 2 3 4 5   08 07 06 05 04

BITSY'S
HARVEST
PARTY

MELODY CARLSON

Illustrations by Susan Reagan

BROADMAN & HOLMAN PUBLISHERS   &   NASHVILLE, TENNESSEE

"Oh, my!" said Bitsy Spider as she scurried across the red and gold carpet of leaves. "The

chill of autumn is in the air and I must find a house to keep me warm during winter."

She walked and she hunted. And she hunted and she walked. And finally, Bitsy Spider

found the perfect home. It was big and orange and round like a ball.

"My favorite color!" she said as she stepped inside the pumpkin and looked around.

"It's perfect!"

Bitsy spun pretty curtains and tablecloths for her pumpkin house.

She found all sorts of lovely things to make it cozy and nice.

It didn't take long before Bitsy Spider was comfortable in her new home.

"Ah," said Bitsy. "Home sweet pumpkin!"

Now that Bitsy Spider was happily settled,

she had a fantastic idea.

"I will have a party!" she exclaimed one morning.

"It will be a Harvest Party.

I will invite all of my dearest friends to my new pumpkin house."

She immediately went to work writing the invitations.

And her penmanship was lovely.

Martha
Spider

Perfect
Entertaining

Party Do's and Dont's...
Proper Placesettings
Uninvited Guests
Table Manners

Spinning out
of control?
Keep it together

arkling web-sites

After sending out the invitations,

Bitsy Spider didn't know what to do next.

"I should make some party plans," she said.

"But where do I begin?"

Since Bitsy had never given a party before,

she decided to consult her *Martha Spider* book on entertaining.

But the more Bitsy read, the more confused she became.

"Parties can be complicated," she said as she set the book aside.

"I will ask my friends for advice," said Bitsy Spider.

"I'm sure they'll have some good party tips."

So Bitsy went over to Widow Mary's house.

"What do you think makes a good party?" asked Bitsy.

"The food, of course," said Widow Mary as she stirred a simmering pot on the stove.

"Everyone knows that a good party must have good food."

Bitsy thanked Widow Mary and continued.

Unfortunately, Bitsy wasn't a very good cook and she knew that she

would be hopeless at making good party food.

Next Bitsy Spider went to Daddy Long Legs' house and knocked on his door.

"What do you think makes a good party?", she asked.

Daddy Long Legs rubbed his chin and thought for a moment.

"Well, I'd have to say that good decorations make for a good party."

Bitsy nodded and thanked him then continued on her way. But as she walked she worried.

Bitsy wasn't good at making decorations. Not like Daddy Long Legs. Why, his house had

looked like something right out of her *Martha Spider* decorating book!

Bitsy went to see her friend Spook next.

"Hi, Spook," she said after recovering from the shock of seeing him leap

from his roof to greet her. "What's hopping?" asked Spook.

"I want to know what you think makes for a good party," she said.

Spook just laughed. "That's easy.

You need good fun and games to have a good party," he told her.

"Everybody knows that."

So Bitsy thanked him and continued on her way. But she felt worse than ever.

She was terrible at planning games.

Next, Bitsy stopped at Wolfgang's house.

She found him playing a banjo, a harmonica, and drums. All at the same time!

"Hi, Wolfie," called Bitsy. "I have a quick question for you.

What do you think makes for a good party?"

He smiled. "Naturally, I think good music always makes a good party."

Bitsy nodded and thanked him and turned back toward home.

"Music?" she said to herself. "I don't play an instrument and everyone knows

I can't even carry a tune. Oh, dear, what will I do?"

19

By the time Bitsy got back home to her sweet pumpkin house

she was completely discouraged.

"I am so foolish to think that I could give a party," she decided.

"I must tell all my friends that the Harvest Party is cancelled."

So Bitsy gathered her friends and announced the sad news.

"I am so sorry, but I must cancel the party," she told them.

"I made a big mistake. Please, forgive me."

Bitsy Spider sadly walked back home. All by herself, she sat in her pumpkin house.

"I was such a silly spider to think I could host a Harvest Party," she said.

"I'm not a good cook. I'm not good at making party decorations.

I don't know a single party game.

And I'm not the least bit talented at music. Oh, dear, what was I thinking?"

Bitsy jumped as someone knocked on her door.

She opened it and all her spider friends began pouring in.

They were bringing all kinds of things and they had on their party clothes.

"Here we are!" they called as they happily filled her pumpkin house.

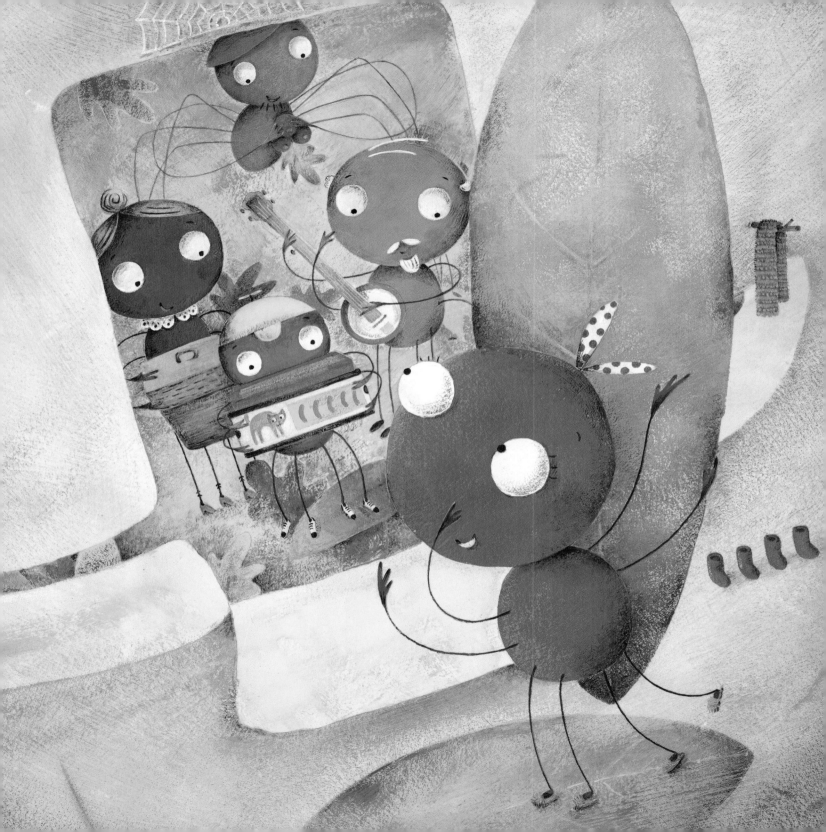

"I brought food!" said Widow Mary as she held up a big picnic basket.

"And I brought decorations," said Daddy Long Legs as he held out a box.

Within minutes, Bitsy's house began to look and smell just like a

Harvest Party should be.

Before long, Spook got everyone to join in for his favorite party games.

They played Pin the Tail on the Cat,

Musical Mushrooms, and even bobbed for berries.

And after the games were finished,

Wolfgang pulled out his instruments and led everyone

in a rousing sing-a-long. It was such fun!

Finally, the party came to an end, and everyone happily thanked Bitsy Spider for having

"the best Harvest Party ever!"

"But it wasn't me," Bitsy said, feeling a bit silly. "I didn't even do anything."

"That's not true," said Widow Mary.

"You're the one who opened your home to your friends."

"That's right," agreed Spook. "And the fun just followed."

Daddy Long Legs nodded. "We wouldn't have had a party without you, Bitsy."

"Yes," said Wolfgang. "You gave us a reason to get together."

"I think I finally get it," said Bitsy. "The way to make a really good party is to have some

really good friends!"

Be hospitable to each other...

Each of you has a special gift...

Use it to help others and show God's grace.

1 Peter 4:9-10

(Author's Paraphrase)